Minikin

Written by Stephen Cosgrove
Illustrated by Robin James

A Serendipity™ *Book*

PSS!
PRICE STERN SLOAN

Dedicated to my daughters, Jennifer and Julie. Though we all be older now, there is hope that we are also wiser.

—*Dad* a.k.a. Stephen

Serendipity was a wonderful island filled with wonderful places. There were white sugar-sand beaches ribboned with frothy waves. There were rivers that wound through savanna and swamp like giant snakes twisting up toward the rolling foothills of a most special place for this particular story the lush, green Meadows of Shy.

Here in the meadows, the winds brushed gently over the treetops whispering wishes and wants for all that lived in Serendipity to hear.

Dotted on the gentle slopes of these meadows, like cotton balls on a green patchwork quilt, were the wonderful bobtailed sheep called Woolies. Here the Woolies grazed on clover and the sweet spring grasses that grew wild all over the Meadows of Shy on the island of Serendipity.

Every year, just after winter packed its tired, cold winds and thick, rain-soaked clouds and moved away, there came the spring with a delight of baggage: the warmth of the sun, longer days and shorter nights.

It was in this time of early spring all over the Meadows of Shy that the mama Woolies, called ewes, would begin the birthing of the lambs. These new, fuzzy babies had ears that seemed too big, and legs that seemed too long.

With their shiny noses flaring, smelling the new, sweet smells, the little lambs would take their first shaky steps in a world filled with all sorts of wonders.

It was late in this springtime bright, after it seemed that all the lambs had been born and already were growing, that a lamb—tiny for even a baby—was born. His name was Minikin, and he, like others before, was amazed by all there was to see.

In those first few moments of life, he sat in a patch of blooming flowers and looked out over this world, so new to him.

Because he was the last to be born, Minikin was much smaller than the lambs that had been born before him. Because he was so small, all the other lambs called him names like "little guy", "pee-wee", or "short stuff".

For his part, Minikin hated having the shortest legs and the shortest tail and just plain being the shortest. Most of all, he didn't like the names, not one little bit. It wasn't his fault that he was small. Usually one lamb or the other would bleat out a name like "little cotton ball" or "dust bunny". With his feelings hurt, Minikin would end up playing alone.

One day, after all the other lambs had laughed a bit louder than usual and called him "lil' bitty" and a few other mean names, Minikin, his tail drooped between his legs, trotted back to his mother.

"Baaa-Mom!" he bleated, a tear in his eye. "I don't want to be itty-bitty anymore. When am I going to be baaa-big?"

His mother nuzzled his nose and smiled that special smile that only mama Woolies seemed to smile. "Minikin, oh my sweet Minikin," she answered. "You will be bigger. It just takes time. Be patient, little Woolie, and wait. Soon you will be just as big as the others."

But Minikin didn't want to wait. He wanted to be big now! "There has to baaa- be a way." He pouted as he moved to the edge of the meadow. There just has to be.

It was by accident that he stumbled, quite literally, on a way.

In his frustration, Minikin, wishing he was taller than he was, had tried to jump over a tangle of branches that had fallen to the ground during a winter storm. Not being quite as tall as he wished he was, his back legs got hooked over the branches, and for a moment he was caught.

It was odd, but as he tried to free himself by stretching out, he kind of felt longer and taller. He pulled and tugged, grunting and groaning, hoping against hope that he was stretching himself taller and taller.

Sadly, the best he achieved was to wedge himself onto a branch. He was hopelessly trapped.

"Baaa!" he bleated. "Someone help me, please! Baaa!"

If it could get worse, it did, for it was the older lambs that heard his bleats for help. And help they did. As they pushed and lifted him off the branch, they laughed and again called him names.

"Hey, what's the matter, shrimp?" one of them teased. "Trying to build yourself some stilts out of the sticks?"

"Little bitty Minikin", another bleated. "If he wasn't so short he would have been able to step over the branches instead of trying to crawl through them."

With the little lamb freed, the rest of young herd trotted off, leaving Minikin sobbing to himself. "This is so baaa- bad! I hate being short. There has to be a way to be taller faster."

And a way there was, but not quite the way that you would think.

A few days later, after a spring downpour that drenched the meadow with heavy rain, Minikin found himself standing in mud as he munched some tender green grasses that were growing there. The mud was very sticky and, of course, stuck fast to the bottoms of cloven hooves. He walked about feeling just a bit taller than he was just a moment before.

"Hmm," he thought with a smile. "If a little mud makes me a little taller, then maybe a lot of mud will make me just as tall as the others."

The rest of that morning, he walked from mud patch to mud patch, building layer after layer on his hooves. Soon he was standing nearly twelve sticks taller than he was before.

"A-ha," he laughed as he stumbled clumsily off to find the young herd. "Now I am just as tall as they are. No one will laugh at me ever again!"

But sometimes the well-laid plans of little lambs don't go quite right.

The other Woolies didn't laugh. They couldn't. They were so amazed by how tall Minikin was, or rather appeared to be, that they were speechless, or "baaaless," as the case may be.

Minikin was so proud as he strutted through the morning grasses still dewy from the rain the day before. But the raindrops on the grass began to dissolve the mud on his feet. Worse than worse, it dissolved the mud on just his left front hoof and his left back hoof first. Soon, to the wide-eyed amazement of the other Woolies, he began to lean hard to one side.

Each wobbly step became more and more difficult until he fell to his side in a muddy, muddy mess. Of course, the others laughed and ran away.

It was his mother who again came to the rescue. As she licked his wool clean, she whispered, "It's only a matter of time, Minikin. Just eat and drink, and with a little patience you will grow as big as the others."

Minikin had little patience, but now with the help of his mother, he had a big plan, indeed!

Eating, he bleated happily as he waded into a knee-deep patch of grass. "If eating will make me taller, then eat I will."

And eat he did.

He ate grass and clover and flowers and ferns. Why, he even tried to eat the bark from the trees, but that was far too bitter. Grass was better.

He ate and he ate for days that turned into weeks, and amazingly he did grow, but not quite the way he had hoped.

Instead of growing taller faster, he grew fatter faster. In fact, his little belly was swollen with so many meals and between-meal snacks and mid-meal munchings that he had eaten himself sick.

He was no taller, but he was a bit wider, and now the thought of clumps of clover made him feel greener than the grass he was eating.

This was very baaa-bad!

It was by accident that Minikin actually began to forget how short he was and, more importantly, that it didn't matter. He had eaten so much that he had become fat, and the only way to lose the weight he had gained trying to grow tall was to play the plump away. So he ran and jumped and played with the others.

He chased and was chased in all sorts of Woolie games, and in the process he forgot that he was short or that they were tall. He was a sheep, and they were sheep, and together they were having a whole lot of fun.

Just as mama Woolie had said, "With a little patience, you will grow." And grow he did.

Minikin was never the biggest. In fact, it was quite possible that he was the smallest always. But more important, he was who he was and he was happy that way in the Meadows of Shy on the island of Serendipity.

IF YOU'RE SMALL, NOT VERY TALL,

PLEASE DON'T THROW A FIT.

REMEMBER A LAMB CALLED MINIKIN,

WHO, IN TIME,

GREW JUST A LITTLE BIT.

Serendipity™ Books

Created by
Stephen Cosgrove and Robin James

Enjoy all the delightful books in the Serendipity™ Series:

Available wherever books are sold.

PRICE STERN SLOAN